There's a Hole in my Garden

Written and Illustrated by
James Stewart

www.av2books.com

Your AV² Media Enhanced book gives you a fiction readalong online. Log on to www.av2books.com and enter the unique book code from this page to use your readalong.

AV² Readalong Navigation

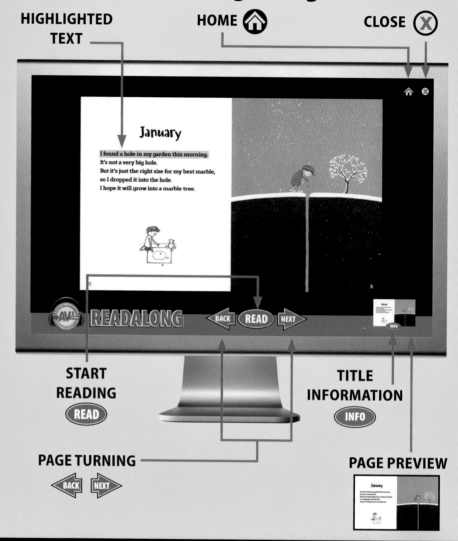

HIGHLIGHTED TEXT

HOME

CLOSE

START READING
READ

TITLE INFORMATION
INFO

PAGE TURNING
BACK NEXT

PAGE PREVIEW

Go to www.av2books.com, and enter this book's unique code.

BOOK CODE

A V M 8 8 7 3 3

AV² by Weigl brings you media enhanced books that support active learning.

First Published by

ALBERT WHITMAN & COMPANY
Publishing children's books since 1919

Published by AV² by Weigl
350 5ᵗʰ Avenue, 59ᵗʰ Floor New York, NY 10118
Website: www.av2books.com

Printed in Guangzhou, China
1 2 3 4 5 6 7 8 9 0 23 22 21 20 19

022019
121118

Library of Congress Control Number: 2019933075

ISBN 978-1-7911-0704-8 (hardcover)
ISBN 978-1-7911-0706-2 (single-user eBook)
ISBN 978-1-7911-0705-5 (multi-user eBook)

Text and illustrations copyright ©2018 by James Stewart
First published in 2018 by Albert Whitman & Company.

There's a Hole in my Garden

January

I found a hole in my garden this morning.

It's not a very big hole.

But it's just the right size for my best marble,

so I dropped it into the hole.

I hope it will grow into a marble tree.

February

Marble trees don't grow overnight.

This one doesn't look like it's growing at all.

But the hole is—it's a little bigger now.

Maybe some candy will grow.

So I bought some and dropped it into the hole.

I hope it will grow into a candy tree.

March

The candy tree isn't growing either.
But the hole is now big enough for
my flashlight.
When I dropped it into the hole, it fell
down and down until I couldn't see the
light anymore.
I hope a flashlight tree will grow and
fill up the hole.

April

No luck with the flashlight tree.
But the hole is now big enough that
my robot went straight in. I'm sorry
I don't have it anymore, but if I get a
robot tree, it will be great.

May

No robot tree.

Just a really big hole.

I put in the piano.

Do piano trees grow?

I'm going to find out.

June

It looks like piano trees don't grow.

All I've got now is a bigger hole.

The dinosaur went straight in, no problem.

Soon I'll have a dinosaur tree.

July

There's no dinosaur tree.
But there is a really big hole.
That train drove right in.

August

You guessed it.

No train tree.

The hole is really big.

Big enough for a ship.

There might be a ship tree soon.

September

No ship tree.
The hole is so big that
I could put a house in it.
So that's what I did.

October

No house tree, but the hole is HUGE.

It took the rocket, no problem.

A rocket tree would fill up that hole.

November

The hole has swallowed the garden.
I never knew a hole could be that big.
It wasn't easy, but in one month
there may be a moon tree
where the garden used to be.

December

No marble tree, no candy tree, no flashlight tree,
no robot tree, no piano tree, no dinosaur tree,
no train tree, no ship tree, no house tree,
no rocket tree, no moon tree.
Just the biggest hole in the world.
I looked in a book to figure out what to do.
The only thing that fits in a black hole is a star.
So that's what I did.
I caught the biggest star I could
and dropped it down that hole.
I can't wait to see my star tree.